ROVER TO THE RESCUE!

HarperFestival is an
imprint of HarperCollins Publishers.
Planet 51: Rover to the Rescue!

Printed in the United States of America.

www.harpercollinschildrens.com
Library of Congress catalog card number: 2009928954
ISBN 978-0-06-184417-1

Typography by Joe Merkel
09 10 11 12 13 UG 10 9 8 7 6 5 4 3 2 1
❖
First Edition

PLANET 51™

ROVER TO THE RESCUE!

Adapted by Ray Santos

HARPER FESTIVAL
An Imprint of HarperCollinsPublishers

There once was a little robot named Rover. Rover was sent on a very important mission. He was sent across space to Planet 51 to take pictures of the planet.

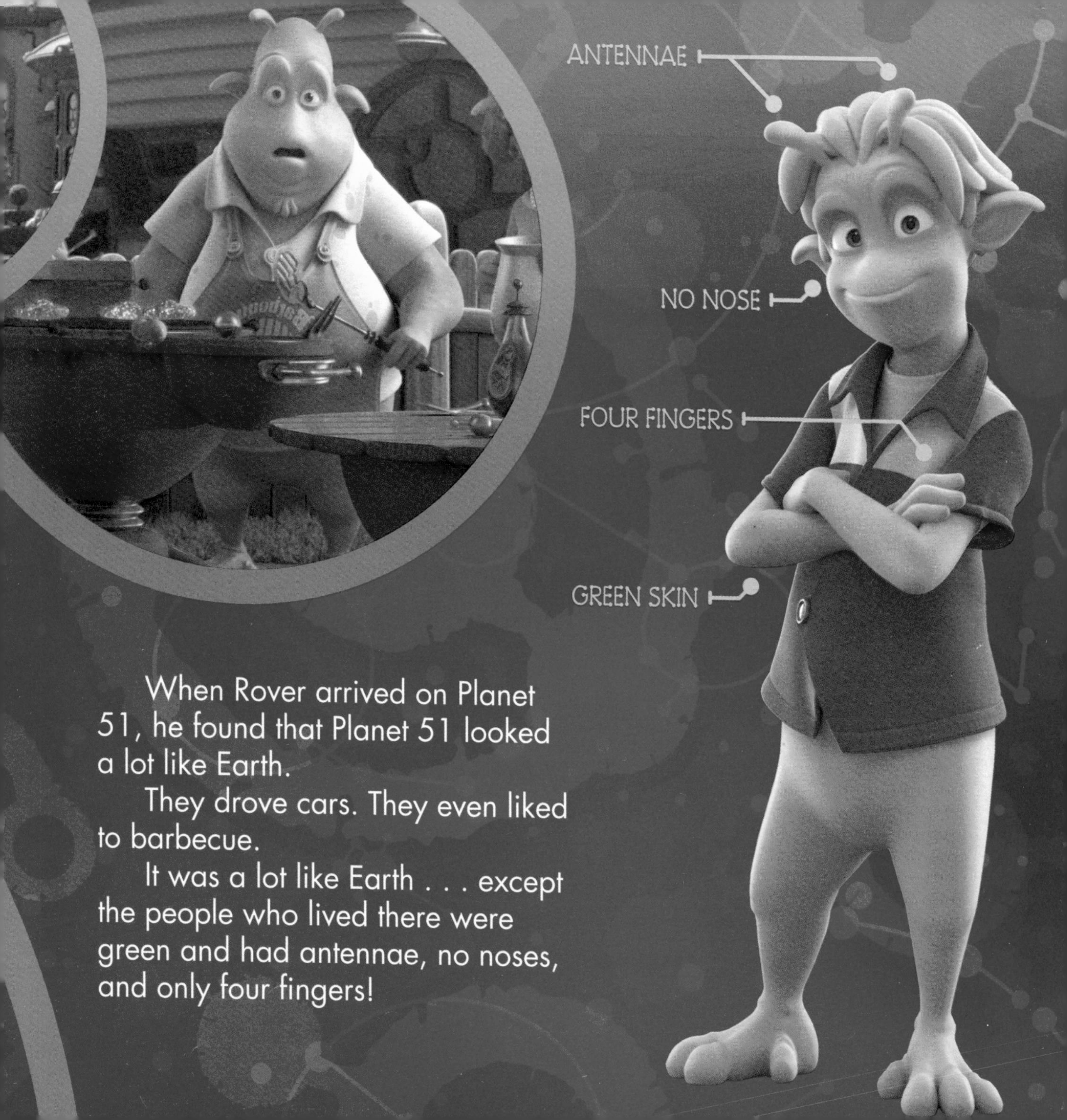

When Rover arrived on Planet 51, he found that Planet 51 looked a lot like Earth.

They drove cars. They even liked to barbecue.

It was a lot like Earth . . . except the people who lived there were green and had antennae, no noses, and only four fingers!

Of course, Rover didn't send pictures of any of that back to Earth. That wasn't his job! Instead he took samples of rocks and pictures of the landscape.

So when astronaut Chuck Baker landed on Planet 51—boy, was Chuck surprised!

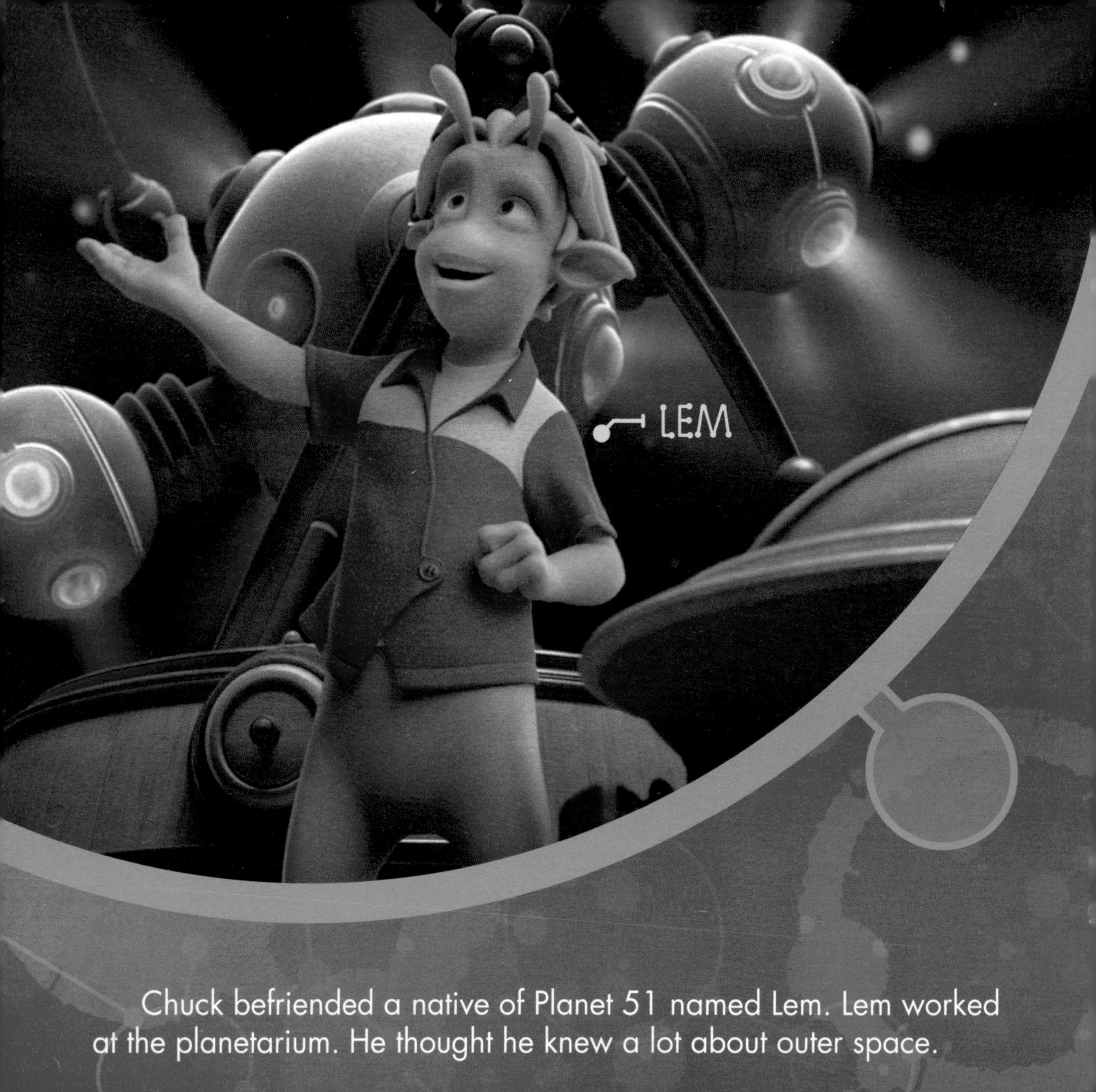

Chuck befriended a native of Planet 51 named Lem. Lem worked at the planetarium. He thought he knew a lot about outer space.

Lem had two best friends, Skiff and Eckle.

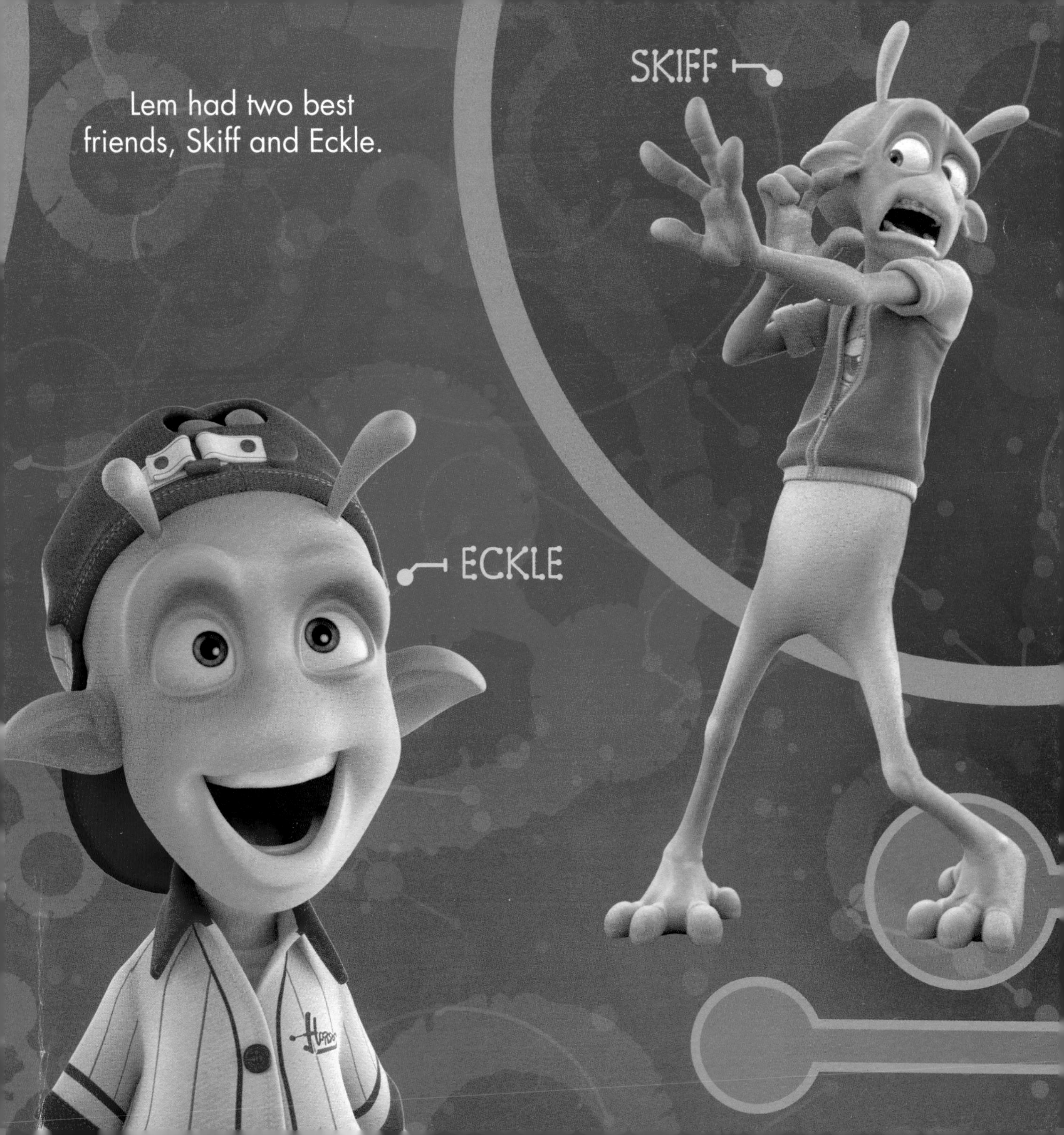

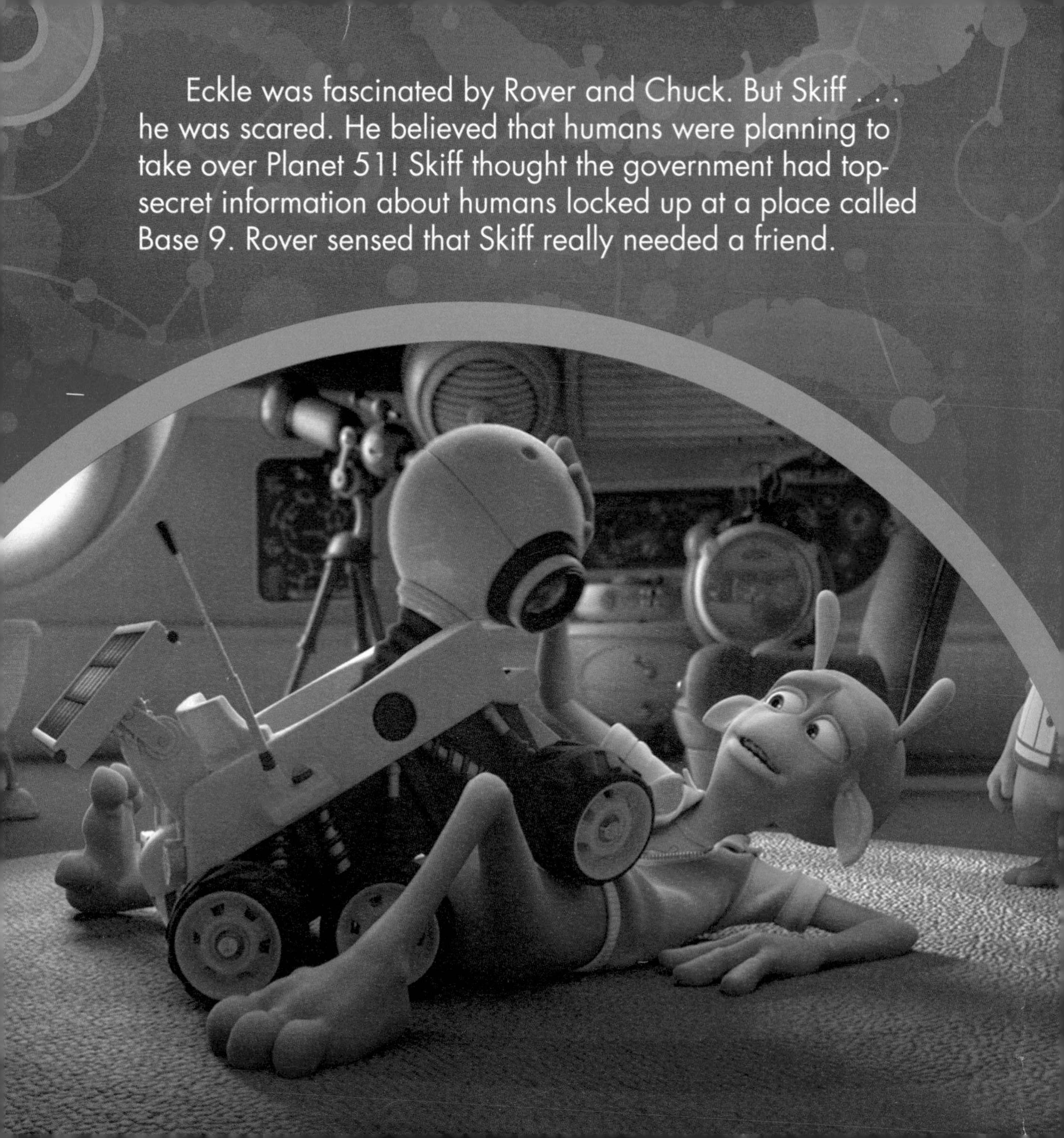

Eckle was fascinated by Rover and Chuck. But Skiff . . . he was scared. He believed that humans were planning to take over Planet 51! Skiff thought the government had top-secret information about humans locked up at a place called Base 9. Rover sensed that Skiff really needed a friend.

Unfortunately, not all the natives of Planet 51 were as friendly as Lem, Skiff, and Eckle. When the army found out about Chuck's landing, it went on high alert. That was when Chuck and Rover knew it was time to go back to Earth.

Rover and Chuck tried to get back to their ship.
But no luck! Chuck was captured and taken away!

Lem, Skiff, and Eckle had no idea where the army took Chuck.
"Rover?" Lem asked the robot. "Can you find Chuck?"
BEEP! BEEP! BEEP! Rover could track Chuck's signal!

Rover's sensors were able to pick up a signal from Chuck's space suit. The gang followed the signal far out of town.

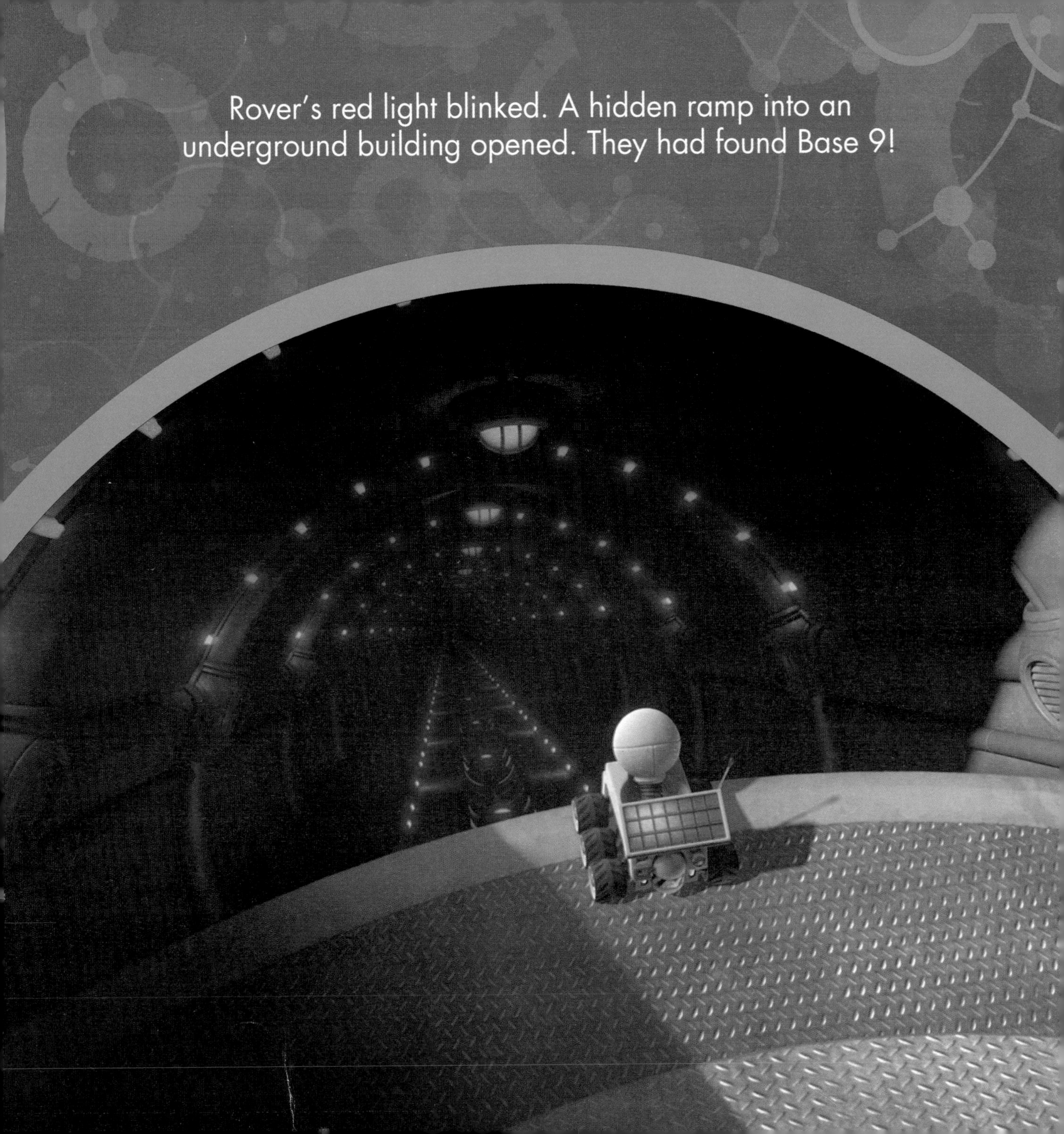

Rover's red light blinked. A hidden ramp into an underground building opened. They had found Base 9!

Lem, Skiff, and Eckle tiptoed behind Rover as he tracked Chuck's signal through a maze of hallways to an open air vent. They shimmied through air ducts until Rover finally stopped at a vent right over Chuck.

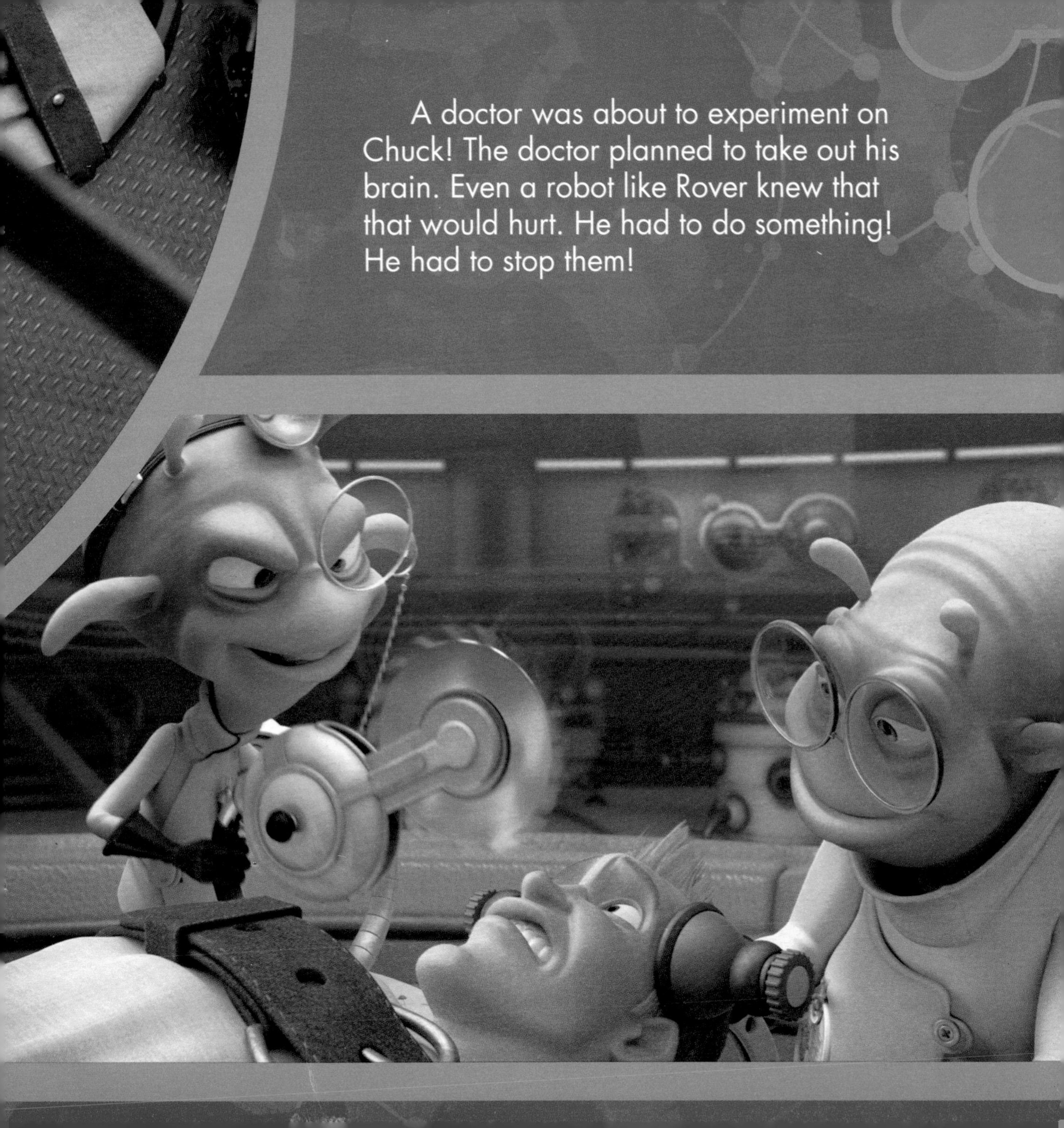

A doctor was about to experiment on Chuck! The doctor planned to take out his brain. Even a robot like Rover knew that that would hurt. He had to do something! He had to stop them!

Rover and his friends broke through the ceiling. They stopped the doctor in the nick of time!

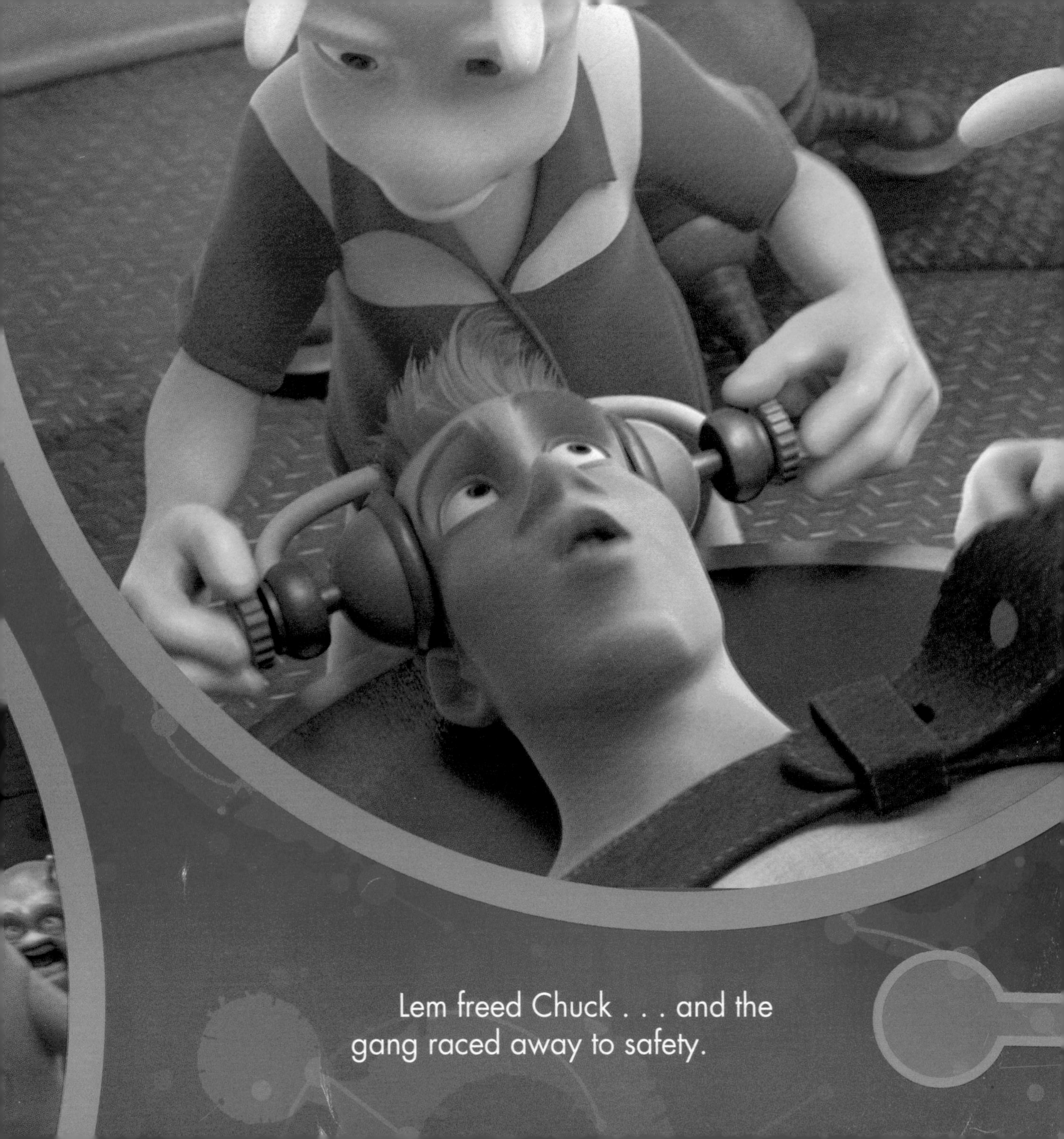

Lem freed Chuck . . . and the gang raced away to safety.

Chuck's mission was over, and he could finally go home. He said good-bye and even gave Lem a big hug.

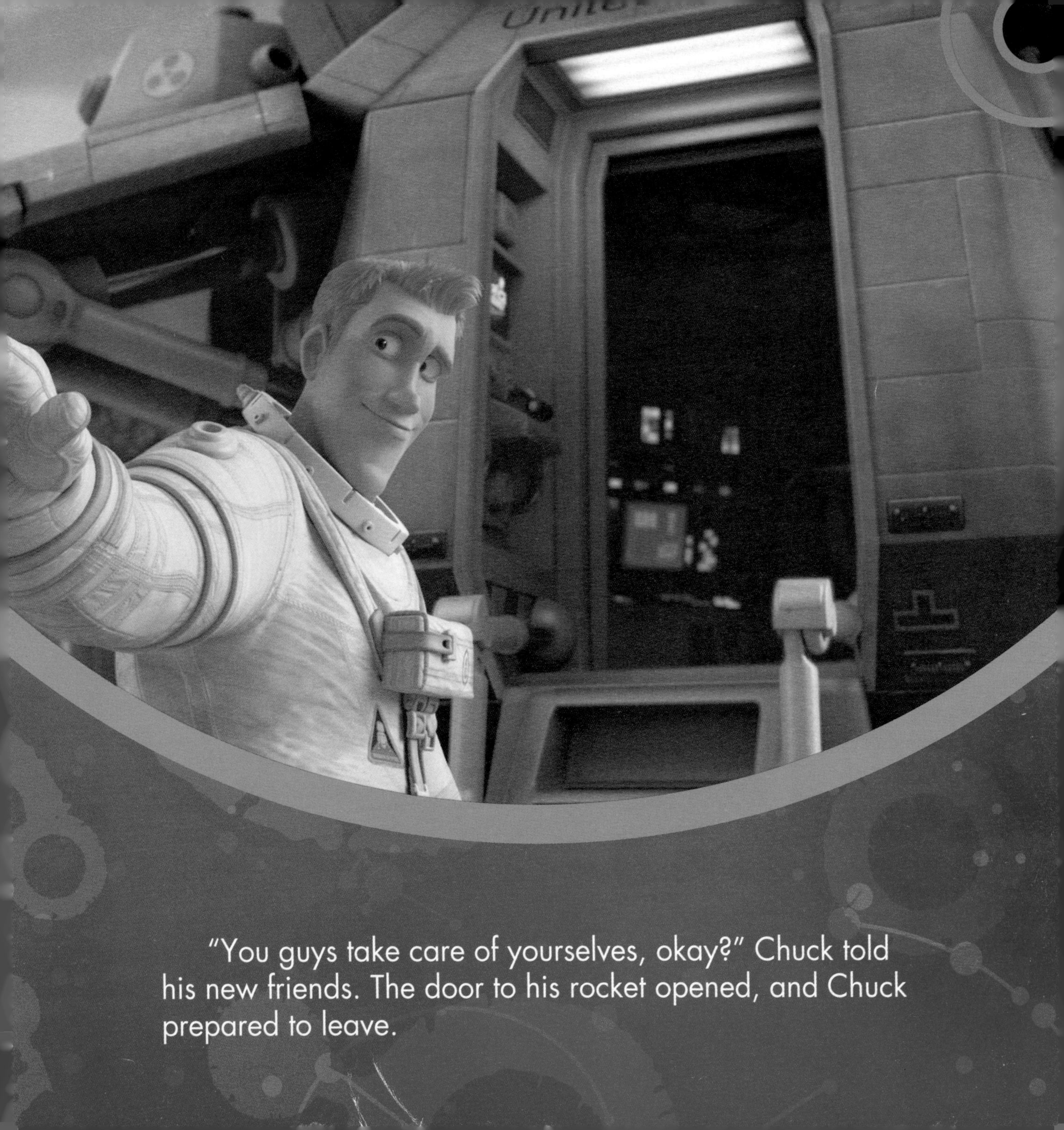

"You guys take care of yourselves, okay?" Chuck told his new friends. The door to his rocket opened, and Chuck prepared to leave.

"Rover, are you coming or do you want to stay here?" Chuck asked. The robot rolled over to Skiff. Chuck knew that Rover wanted to stay. "He needs oil every three thousand miles," he told the natives of Planet 51 as he waved good-bye. "And a lot of love."

Rover watched as Chuck's ship took off. The robot was sad to see Chuck leave, but he was happy that he had so many new friends.